The Case of the
Mummy Mystery

Read all the Jigsaw Jones Mysteries

Coming Soon

The Case of the Mummy Mystery

by James Preller

illustrated by John Speirs

cover illustration by R. W. Alley

A
LITTLE APPLE
PAPERBACK

SCHOLASTIC INC.
New York Toronto London Auckland Sydney
Mexico City New Delhi Hong Kong

To my editor, Helen Perelman
— for loving Jigsaw from the beginning,
for believing in mummies,
for putting up with me,
and for correcting my mistakes.
(Not that I ever make any.)

Yeesh!
~HP

Book design by Dawn Adelman

ISBN 0-439-08094-0

12 11 10 9 8 7 6 5 4 3 2 1   0 1 2 3 4/0

Printed in the U.S.A.   40
First Scholastic printing, September 1999

CONTENTS

Chapter One
Guess He'll Go Eat Worms

I'm a detective, and I solve mysteries.

Some cases are nice and easy. Somebody loses a cat. I find the cat. They pay me, and everybody's as happy as a bug in a rug.

Then there are the tough cases. The cases that wiggle and turn like a worm on a hook. The mysteries that are full of surprises.

This was one of those cases.

I *thought* it was going to be a simple job. But one thing's for sure. I never expected mummy trouble.

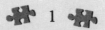 1

That's right. I said mummy. Not mommy. *Mummy.*

Mommies I can handle. *Mummies* are a different story. A mummy is a walking zombie. He's a guy covered with bandages who looks like he jumped off a tall building without a parachute. He's a guy who was dead and buried — but then came back to walk the earth.

That kind of mummy.

Yeesh.

It all started with a dare. At least that's the way Joey Pignattano told it. We were in my office, a tree house in my backyard. As usual, Joey Pignattano's mouth was moving. But I couldn't believe what my ears were hearing.

I glanced at my best friend and partner, Mila Yeh. Her arms were folded across her stomach. Her face looked pale, like she was going to be sick. As Joey talked, Mila's eyes

blinked open and closed, open and closed, like the flashing lights of a Christmas tree.

Mila couldn't believe what Joey was saying, either.

I interrupted Joey, speaking slowly and carefully. "Hold on, Joey. Let me make sure I've got all the facts." I read from my detective journal. "You are telling us that you are going to eat . . . a worm."

Joey's head bobbed up and down enthusiastically. "For a dollar," he added, smiling proudly.

"For a dollar," I repeated. "Well, that's not something you see every day." I scratched the back of my neck. "Are you going to eat it plain? Or with ketchup?"

Joey's eyes got wide. "Great idea!" he exclaimed. "I never thought of ketchup!"

"It's something to think about," I told him.

Mila shot me a look. I ignored her and

continued. "Are you going to swallow the worm whole? Or chew on it?"

Joey bit his lip. "Dunno," he said. "Depends on the worm."

Mila looked at us like we were both nuts. But I had to admit. I sort of liked the idea of Joey Pignattano eating a worm. Like I said before, it's not something you see every day.

"Wait a minute," Mila said. "Who is paying you the dollar?"

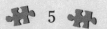 5

"Bobby Solofsky," Joey answered.

"When are you eating the worm?" she asked.

"Friday," Joey said.

"That's Halloween," I said.

Joey nodded. It sure was.

Mila just shook her head. "Don't you think that eating a worm is sort of . . . gross?"

Joey shrugged happily. He didn't particularly think so.

"So why do you need a detective?" I said.

Joey leaned close. "I don't want to get cheated," he whispered. "I don't trust Bobby — he's trouble."

I wouldn't trust Bobby Solofsky, either. But then again, I wouldn't eat a worm for a dollar. I guess there are two kinds of people in the world. Some eat worms. The others, well, they just don't.

Picky eaters, I guess.

"I could make sure you don't get

cheated," I assured him. "But I make a dollar a day. Can you afford me?"

Joey stared hard into my eyes. "Would I eat a worm if I had that kind of money?" he asked.

I saw his point. Joey Pignattano was flat broke. "OK, Joey," I said. "You can owe me."

So that's how this whole mess started.

The mummy didn't come into it until later on.

Chapter Two
Not Hungry

That night before dinner, my brothers Daniel and Nicholas were messing around in the playroom while I did my spelling homework. I had to write each word five times and put them in ABC order.

Black   Halloween
Candy   ~~Pumpkin~~
Children   October
Frightened   Pumpkin
Ghost   Spooky
~~Frightened~~ Treat

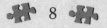

While I worked, I listened to my brothers talk. "Every Halloween," Daniel said to Nicholas, "he prowls through town, causing trouble everywhere he goes."

I looked up from my homework. "Who does?" I asked.

"And he eats stray cats," Daniel said.

"Who does?" I asked again.

"And he loves mischief," Daniel said.

"GUYS!" I yelled. "WHO loves mischief?"

"Don't tell him," Nicholas said. "He'll have bad dreams."

"Tell me WHAT?" I demanded.

"Nothing," Daniel answered.

"Please," I pleaded. "What are you guys talking about?"

Daniel sighed. "OK. But you have to promise not to tell Mom and Dad."

"I promise," I said.

"Do you promise on a stack of Batman comic books?" Nicholas asked.

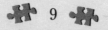

"I promise," I repeated. "Now tell me: *What are you guys talking about?!*"

Daniel looked around cautiously. "Not here," he said. "Down in the basement."

Suddenly, my mother called out, "Dinner's almost ready. Theodore, it's your turn to set the table."

"MOM!" I complained. "Please don't call me Theodore. Everybody calls me Jigsaw."

My dad came into the room. In a funny voice he said, "I don't care WHAT you call me . . . as long as you call me for dinner."

Then he gave my mom a big, sloppy kiss. Oh, brother.

Daniel gave me a poke. "After dinner," he whispered. "In the basement."

I smiled. Secrets are almost as much fun as mysteries.

My mom set out a big, steaming bowl of spaghetti and meat sauce. "Joey Pignattano is going to eat a worm for a dollar," I announced.

"That's very nice, dear," my mother said. "Please pass the spaghetti, Billy."

I continued, "I wouldn't eat a worm, no matter how much you paid me."

"I'm proud of you, son," my father mumbled.

I stared down at my plate of spaghetti. "I think Joey is crazy. Worms are so slippery and slimy and gross." I put down my knife and fork. "Sort of like, er, spaghetti."

"Jigsaw!" my sister, Hillary, protested. "Gross me out the door!" She spit out something into her napkin.

"Hey, hey," my father said. "No talk of worms at the dinner table."

One by one, my brothers pushed their plates away.

"What's wrong?" my mom asked.

Billy frowned at me. "Sorry, Mom," he said. "I just don't feel hungry anymore."

"Me, neither," Daniel and Nicholas said.

Hillary complained, "All this talk about eating worms has spoiled my appetite — *especially* for spaghetti."

Grams didn't seem to pay any attention. She just kept shoveling huge forkfuls into her mouth. Grams finally winked and said, "Eat up, kids. These worms are delicious."

Chapter Three
The Legend of the Mummy

An hour later, I followed Daniel and Nicholas down into the basement. My oldest brother, Billy, was already down there. He was rebuilding an old car engine. His face was marked with black grease. A million different parts were laid out on newspaper.

Billy looked up from unscrewing some kind of whatcha-ma-call-it. "What's up?"

"We're going to tell Jigsaw about the Halloween legend," Daniel explained. "You know — the mummy."

Billy nodded slowly, staring hard at Daniel. "Oh, yeah," he said. "The mummy. Don't you think it might scare him too much? I mean, he's only a pip-squeak."

"Am not," I protested.

Daniel sighed. "OK, OK. You know what a mummy is, right?"

"Sure," I joked. "He's like Frankenstein's cousin. Or nephew, or something."

They laughed at me.

"Hey, I'm kidding," I said. "A mummy is a movie monster. He was in one of my puzzles, 'The Monsters of Hollywood.'"

Daniel shook his head. "Yeah, but this one is real, and he lives right here in town."

"Yeah," Billy said. "The mummy rises from his wormy grave and comes alive every Halloween."

Billy got up, arms outstretched, and walked stiffly across the room. He moaned and groaned. He tried to grab me by the throat. But I ducked out of the way.

"Remember Mrs. Estep's cat, Twinkles?" Daniel asked.

I remembered.

"Remember how it disappeared two years ago at Halloween?"

I still remembered.

"The mummy got it," Billy said.

"How do you know?" I asked.

"Barney Fodstock saw it happen," Daniel said.

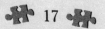

Billy went on, "And you know Mr. Reilly, the old guy with white hair who lives on Charlie's Hill? His hair used to be jet-black."

"So?"

"So his hair turned completely white in one night," Billy said. "Because he saw the mummy and nearly died of fright."

A chill ran down my spine. Which was weird, because I didn't really — *really, really* — believe in mummies.

But still, it was hard to know for sure.

Chapter Four

It's a Mystery

When I got to the bus stop the next morning, I found Joey Pignattano staring into his hand.

"What are you doing, Joey?" I asked.

"Training," he answered.

I looked closer. An ant crawled on Joey's palm.

Joey closed his eyes, brought his hand to his mouth, and swallowed. The poor ant never knew what hit him. One minute he was crawling around, searching for a

crumb. The next minute the little guy was trapped inside Joey Pignattano's belly.

What a way to go.

Joey licked his lips and shrugged. "Not so bad," he said.

"Sure," I said. "Better than Raisinets. But a tiny ant is not exactly a squishy worm."

"I know," Joey said earnestly. "I'm working my way up the animal kingdom."

Yeesh.

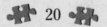

Mila skipped out of her house. The minute she saw Joey, Mila started singing:

"Nobody likes me,
Everybody hates me,
Guess I'll go eat worms.
First you peel the skin off,
Then you chew the guts up,
Ooey-gooey wooorms!"

When the bus pulled away, I watched as Mila's house got smaller and smaller until it was the size of a bug. "Did you decide yet what you're going to be for Halloween?" Mila asked me.

I shrugged. "I don't know. A pirate, I guess. Or maybe a gorilla. Or Frankenstein, I think, maybe. How about you?" I asked.

Mila smiled. "Here's a hint. *I vant to suck your blood!"*

We both laughed. Mila was going to be a vampire. "My stepmom, Alice, is sewing me this really cool black cape. And I already have a set of plastic fangs."

Then I told her what my brothers had told me. About the mummy . . . and how he walks through town on Halloween . . . and causes all sorts of trouble.

Ralphie Jordan, who was sitting in front of us, turned around. "It's true," he said. "Barney Fodstock even saw the mummy with his own eyes."

"How do YOU know?" I asked.

"Everybody knows about the mummy," Ralphie said. "It knocked down Earl Bartholemew last year."

Earl Bartholemew was an eighth-grader who lived across the street from Ralphie. "Are you sure?"

Ralphie's eyes lit up, bright and large. "It was Halloween night. Earl was in a hurry, so he cut through Greenlawn Cemetery. Suddenly, he felt someone push him in the back. Earl fell and chipped a tooth. But

when he turned around . . . no one was there."

"Maybe he tripped," I said.

Ralphie shook his head. "No, Jigsaw. He was *pushed*."

"Well," Mila said, pulling on her long black hair, "it sounds like a mystery to me."

I pulled out my detective journal. I turned to a new page. With an orange marker, I wrote: **THE CASE OF THE MUMMY MYSTERY**. "This looks like a job for Jigsaw Jones, Private Eye."

Chapter Five

Halloween Fever

Halloween was nearly here. Everybody in room 201 was ready to explode with excitement. Our teacher, Ms. Gleason, said she was going to send the whole class to the nurse. "You kids have a bad case of Halloween Fever."

We sure did. We were really looking forward to the Halloween parade. All the parents were going to come. Even Grams. And it was the same day that Joey Pignattano was going to eat a worm. What more could you ask for?

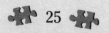

Meanwhile, the story of the Halloween mummy swept through the class like a hurricane. The more kids talked about it, the better the stories got. Now even Bobby Solofsky claimed that he had seen the mummy. I didn't know about that. But one thing was sure: We were all going to stay far away from Greenlawn Cemetery.

Ms. Gleason was excited, too. But she wasn't thinking about mummies. "I really want to win the teachers' pumpkin pie contest this year," she told us. "Ever since last year's disaster, I've been working extra hard in the kitchen."

"What happened last year?" Danika Starling asked.

Ms. Gleason buried her face in her hands. "I left my pie on the radiator at school on the day of the contest. By the time the judge saw it, my beautiful pie was melting. You could have eaten it with a straw!"

Then Ms. Gleason cheered up. "But this

is my year," she said. "I'm going to make the most beautiful, most delicious pumpkin pie this school has ever seen — and I'm *not* going to leave it on the radiator!"

"I don't like pumpkin pie," complained Athena Lorenzo. She squinched up her face. "It tastes too . . . *pumpkiny*."

Ms. Gleason walked to the blackboard. "Well, OK, then. Everyone break into groups. We've got a lot of work to do."

Ms. Gleason was the best teacher in

the school. She made learning fun. This week's theme was Halloween. All week long, every activity had something to do with Halloween. So we didn't even mind learning.

On Monday, Ms. Gleason draped a white sheet over the big stuffed chair for story hour. She drew two black eyes on the sheet. We all took turns sitting in the ghost's lap for story hour. Even better, we read spooky stories every day.

On Tuesday, we played Halloween Bingo with our vocabulary words. We did Spider Math on Wednesday. Every group got a spider s body with a different number on it. My group   Mila, Joey, Geetha Nair, and me   got number seventeen. Then we had to pick out the legs that added up to seventeen and attach them to the body. I attached 9 + 8 and 19 - 2. Joey Pignattano tried to attach 1 + 7, but Mila wouldn t let him. In art, we made really cool bat mobiles.

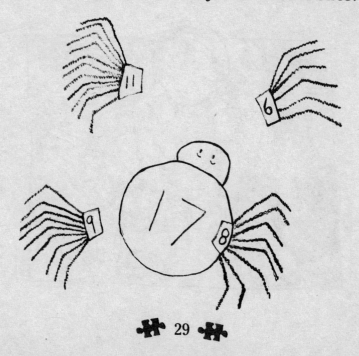

Meanwhile, I did a little work on Joey's case. First I caught up with Bobby Solofsky in the cafeteria. He was sitting with Bigs Maloney, Lucy Hiller, and Eddie Becker. "Joey told me about your dare," I said.

Bobby slid his tongue across his teeth and made a sucking noise. "Yeah, so what," he said.

"I'm supposed to make sure everything's fair and square," I told him. "Joey doesn't want to get cheated."

"Cheated?! *By me?!*" Bobby placed his hand on his chest. "I'd never cheat anyone."

"Sure, Solofsky," I said. "You're a regular Boy Scout. But just in case, why don't you let me hold onto the money. This way it won't get lost."

Bobby shook his head. "Aw, Theodore," he said — Bobby called me Theodore just to bug me — "you can trust me."

"Sure I can," I replied. "But I don't. I'll be watching you, Solofsky. You better not try any funny business."

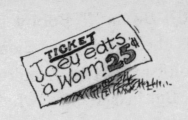

Chapter Six

Eddie's Big Idea

Eddie Becker pulled me aside after lunch. "Hey, Jigsaw," he said. "Is Joey really going to eat a worm for a dollar?"

I shrugged. "You know Joey. What do *you* think?"

Eddie smiled. "I think he's crazy enough to do it."

I nodded. Joey was *definitely* crazy enough to do it.

"But you're going about this the wrong way," Eddie said. "He could make a lot more than a dollar if you let me help."

"How?" I asked.

"Sell tickets," Eddie said. "I bet you a lot of kids would pay a quarter to watch him do it."

I thought it over. "Well, it's not something you see every day."

Eddie offered to be in charge of selling tickets. "But I want pay for my work," he said. "I get half. Joey gets half."

It was a deal. We shook hands right there. Now Joey would be able to pay the dollar he owed me.

"One more thing," I added. "Tell Bobby that *I'll* bring the worm."

Back in room 201, I found a note inside my desk. It was in code:

> blue the witch candy purple mummy
> and tall man green is like door monster
> red going brown to trick treat orange
> get black you!

I knew the note was from Mila. She liked to test my brainpower. This one was called a color code. The only words that really mattered were the ones that came right after color words. So I circled all the color words. Then I underlined the words that were next in line.

I looked up and saw Mila smiling at me.

I grabbed my throat and made a choking sound. Then my head fell on the desk, as if I had suddenly dropped dead.

At recess, Ms. Gleason gave Mila and me permission to visit the school library. We wanted to learn more about mummies. We found a good book called *Mummies! Mummies! and More Mummies!*

I was a good reader. But Mila was a fantastic reader. It didn't matter how many words were in the book or how squished together the words were. Mila could read just about anything.

I looked over her shoulder while Mila flipped through the pages. She'd read a little bit, say, "Hmmm," or "Boring," or "Yuck," and flip the page. When she said "Yuck," I always made her read it out loud.

Here's the thing. Long ago in Egypt, they used to make mummies all the time. That's because the Egyptians didn't want the bodies to get all juicy. The Egyptians believed they would need their bodies later on in a place called "The Afterlife." The Afterlife was their idea of heaven.

It took seventy days to make a mummy. The grossest part was when they scooped

out the brain. They did this by sticking a long spoon up the dead guy's nose!

Yeesh.

Then the embalmer — the guy who was in charge of making mummies — took out the dead guy's stomach and guts and stuff. Then they dried the body out with a special salt called natron and wrapped it up nice and tight like a birthday present.

Presto! One mummy, coming up!

Ding! The bell rang. We had to get back to room 201.

Oh, well. At least now I understood why mummies were so grumpy. They've all got headaches!

Chapter Seven

Worms in a Box

Mila came over after school. It was the day before Halloween and we had a lot to do. I went into my garage and got a shovel. "What's that for?" Mila asked.

"Worms," I said.

We went into the backyard and dug for worms. My dog, Rags, watched us closely. I think he was hoping for a bone. I turned over a rock. "Wow, look at all of them!" I exclaimed.

I asked Mila, "Which one looks the yummiest?"

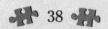

Mila rolled her eyes.

"Joey should choose," I decided. "I'll give him a nice selection. Mila, we need a box or something."

Mila ran inside my house and came back with a square box about three inches tall. "Your dad gave it to me," she said.

I scooped the worms into the box. I tossed in some dirt and rocks, just so they'd feel at home.

That night, I got my costume together and shoved it into my book bag. I put the box of worms into a 3rd Street Food Market bag and went to bed. After I flicked off the light, my door nudged open. *Clomp, clomp, clomp.* Rags climbed into bed with me. I held him tight and fell asleep, dreaming of candy and costumes, worms and mummies.

The next morning it was Halloween. *Finally.* I saw Joey Pignattano at the bus stop. He seemed quiet, nervous. "Are you ready, Joey?"

He nodded solemnly. "I think so," he said.

I patted my grocery bag. "I've got a nice selection of worms for you, Joey. Fat ones, skinny ones, you name it."

Joey stared into the bag. "Can they breathe in there?" he asked.

"Don't worry," I said. "The worms are just fine."

On the bus, Ralphie turned around in his seat and smiled at Mila and me. "I learned a

new poem yesterday." He beamed. "Want to hear it?"

"Not really," I said.

Mila shushed me. "Go ahead, Ralphie."

"My brother, Justin, taught it to me. It's pretty gross," he warned.

"We can take it," Mila said.

"You're supposed to say it when you pass a cemetery," he explained. He looked out the window. There were no graves in sight. "But this is a special occasion."

Ralphie cleared his throat.

"The worms go in, the worms go out.
They crawl in your stomach
And out through your mouth.
Your teeth decay, your body turns gray,
And that's the end of a wonderful day."

The poem was a big hit. Pretty soon, everyone on the bus was repeating it. I

guess you could say we were just a bunch of poetry lovers.

Our plan for Joey was set. He was going to eat the worm during afternoon recess. Eddie Becker said he'd already sold eleven tickets. I took out my journal and figured out the math. Eleven quarters added up to two dollars and seventy-five cents. Now Joey could pay me with Bobby's dollar and still have money left over. Everything seemed perfect.

Then disaster struck.

Chapter Eight

The Robbery!

It never could have happened on a normal school day. But Halloween was anything but normal. "Total chaos," Ms. Gleason called it. And I guess she was right. It wasn't a big day for learning.

"What did you boys and girls have for breakfast this morning?" she asked. "Flubber? You're practically bouncing off the walls."

We all laughed. Ms. Gleason was pretty funny sometimes.

A lot of the kids brought in their

costumes. Some didn't. That's because their parents would pick them up for lunch. They'd go home, eat lunch, and get dressed. Then everyone would hurry back to school for the one o'clock Halloween parade.

I hung my book bag on a hook. Because my cubby was so crowded with junk, I placed my worm bag on the closet floor. Parents started arriving at around eleven o'clock. Everyone complimented Ms. Gleason on her costume. She was dressed up as a basset hound, complete with long ears and white-tipped tail.

I got dressed in the school bathroom right after lunch. It wasn't easy. Fortunately, the janitor, Good Old Mr. Copabianco, helped me draw stitches on my neck and forehead.

"Finished," he finally announced.

I stepped before the mirror.

"Needs blood," I observed.

 45

Mr. Copabianco rubbed his chin thoughtfully. "I've got just the thing," he said, and rushed out the door. He came back whistling. Mr. Copabianco had a can of red paint and a brush in his hand.

He added a few dabs of paint. "Nice and gruesome, Mr. Jones," he said admiringly. Good Old Mr. Copabianco!

I still had plenty of time before the parade. I was glad, because I wanted to check on the worms. Maybe Joey was right. Maybe they did need air.

I went to the closet.

I looked low. I looked high.

But my bag was gone.

Who in the world would steal a box of worms?

Chapter Nine

An Eyewitness

I told Mila that the worms were missing.

We immediately walked over to Bobby Solofsky. "Is this another one of your tricks?" I asked.

Bobby was dressed like a football player. "No tricks, Frankenstein," he replied. "I'm a quarterback. I don't pull bunnies out of my hat. Besides, I don't know what in the world you're talking about."

I watched him closely. Bobby looked me right in the eye when he spoke — and he never blinked. He was telling the truth for a change. Go figure.

"Ms. Gleason, did you see anyone take my bag?"

"No, Theodore, I didn't," she answered. "Today has been so hectic with people coming and going. What kind of bag was it?"

I told her it was a brown bag with red handles.

"Was it from the 3rd Street Food Market?" she asked.

"Yes," I said hopefully.

"I know exactly what it looks like," she said. "I used the same kind of bag for my pie today. I'll keep my eye out for it."

Ms. Gleason greeted Nicole Rodriguez and her mother. Nicole was dressed as a giant grapefruit. Suddenly, Bigs Maloney, dressed like a professional wrestler, entered the room. "Ms. Gleason, I'm back," he announced.

"You found it OK?" Ms. Gleason asked him.

"Easy as pie," Bigs said, smiling widely.

"Jigsaw," Mila said. "If someone took that bag, then there must be witnesses. Let's ask around. Maybe somebody saw the thief."

Mila had better luck than me. She was back in five minutes. "I found a witness," Mila said.

Mila stood beside Helen Zuckerman, who was dressed like Wonder Woman.

I pulled out my journal. "What did you see, Helen?"

"This may sound crazy," she said, "but I saw someone walking down the hall carrying a bag."

"What kind of bag?" I asked.

"Um, brown, with red handles, I think."

"Did you get a good look at who had the bag?" I asked.

Helen glanced at Mila. "Tell him," Mila urged.

"Well, um, sort of."

"Sort of?" I said. "What do you mean, *sort of*?"

Helen looked me in the eye. "I saw him. But at the same time, I didn't see him."

I closed my journal. "Helen, you may be a witness to a crime. Tell me exactly what you saw."

"He was . . . he was a . . . mummy."

"A mummy!" I exclaimed. "Surely you're kidding."

"Don't call me *Shirley*," Helen said.

"Huh?"

"My name is Helen. Don't call me Shirley."

"I DIDN'T call you Shirley," I explained.

"Did too," Helen replied. "You said, 'Shirley, you're kidding.'"

"Shirley?" I said. "No, no. I said *surely*."

"Are you sure?" Helen said, confused.

"Not anymore," I admitted.

Oh, brother. Now we were both confused. I scribbled in my journal: Witness saw mummy with shopping bag.

"Pretty strange," I said.

"I don't know *what's* stranger," Mila observed. "That Helen saw a mummy . . . or the conversation I just heard!"

Chapter Ten

Pumpkin Pie?

I never really believed it. I mean, it was fun to talk about mummies and all that. But I thought it was just talk — just my rotten brothers telling me crazy stories.

But now I didn't know what to think.

Did the mummy really rise from the dead? Was this his idea of Halloween fun? Stealing a bag of worms?

The trouble was, I didn't have enough facts. And you can't solve a mystery without facts. It's like trying to finish a jigsaw puzzle with a few pieces missing.

Just not gonna happen.

"Maybe the worm thing wasn't such a hot idea," Mila said.

"Poor Joey," I said glumly. "It will break his heart. We sold tickets and everything."

Meanwhile, a group of kids was gathered around Helen.

"He's back," I heard Bobby Solofsky say. "The mummy has returned!"

That nearly sent the class into a panic. Ralphie Jordan told everyone about what happened to Twinkles the cat and Earl Bartholemew.

"And don't forget Mr. Reilly," Kim Lewis said. "His hair turned white when he saw the mummy."

The more kids talked, the more afraid they got. A few boys even hid in the closet until Ms. Gleason told them that enough was enough. She barked, "That's enough of this silliness."

Ms. Gleason stood up and slammed the

closet doors shut. Unfortunately, her tail got stuck between the doors. That made her even madder.

That's when Ms. Gleason saw that Geetha Nair was hiding under a desk.

"Geetha, what are you doing under there?"

"Hiding from the mummy," Geetha answered in a quivery voice.

Ms. Gleason heaved a heavy sigh. "Please come out, Geetha. I don't think mummies go to school."

Suddenly, Geetha pointed toward the door and screamed, "THEN WHAT'S HE DOING HERE?!"

Everyone stared at the door. A hand, wrapped in bandages, slowly pushed it open.

Kids screamed and dived under desks.

But I stood my ground. Not because I was brave. But because this particular mummy looked a little familiar.

"Oof," the mummy mumbled as he bumped into Ms. Gleason's desk.

"Joey?" I said. "Is that you?"

The mummy lifted a bandage and looked at me with one eye. "Hey, Jigsaw. Nice costume. It's me, Joey." He looked around the classroom. "Why is everyone under their desks? Did the hamsters get out again?"

I noticed that Joey was holding a bag. *My bag.* I snatched it from his hand. "I've been looking all over for this."

"Hey, don't get mad," Joey said. "Besides, I thought you said there were worms in there."

Bigs and Mila gathered around.

Joey continued, "See, I had been thinking about the worms all day. I was worried about them in that box of yours. So I thought I'd take them outside for a little exercise."

"Exercise?" I said.

"And fresh air," Joey added.

I scratched the back of my neck. "So what's the problem?" I asked.

Joey opened the bag and pulled out a box. It was shaped like my box. Except it was white, not gray. Joey opened the lid. "See for yourself."

I looked inside. "Pie?"

Joey stuck his thumb into the pie and gave it a lick. "Mmmm, pumpkin," he said.

Then I remembered what Ms. Gleason

had said. *She used the same kind of bag for her pie today.*

Mila must have been reading my mind. She said, "But if Joey took Ms. Gleason's pumpkin pie . . . then who has the worms?"

Chapter Eleven

Mila Saves the Day

I turned to Bigs. "Where were you just now, before you came into the classroom?"

Bigs jerked his thumb toward the door. "I delivered a bag for Ms. Gleason. It was for the —"

"— pumpkin pie contest!" Mila shouted, finishing his sentence.

Somehow the bags got switched. Joey took the pie by mistake. And Bigs delivered a box of worms!

Uh-oh.

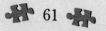

There was no time to waste. "Bigs, Mila, let's go — and bring the pie!"

We raced to the auditorium.

The halls were crowded with ghouls and ghosts. We saw pirates and superheroes, ballerinas and princesses. We saw a giant M&M chatting with Pocahontas. We even saw a four-legged cow. With so much going on, no one paid much attention to a vampire, Frankenstein, and a wrestler hustling down the hall.

Bigs opened the auditorium door a crack.

"What do you see?" Mila asked.

Bigs whispered, "I see the principal, Mr. Rogers, standing in front of a long table. He has a fork in his hand."

"This isn't good," Mila said.

"He's already judging the pie contest," Bigs explained.

We all poked our heads through the crack in the door. Mr. Rogers placed a fork

in his mouth. He chewed thoughtfully. The school secretary, Mrs. Garcia, stood beside him. She wrote on a clipboard.

"Mr. Rogers is at the end of the table, Jigsaw," Bigs said. "He's opening the last box!"

"What can we do now?" Mila asked.

"WAIT!" I screamed.

But it was too late.

We ran up to the table. Mr. Rogers — who, by the way, was dressed like The Cat in the Hat — stared at us. Then down into the box. Then at us again.

He had found the worms.

And we were in big, big trouble.

Mr. Rogers's face turned red. "Is this some kind of foolish prank?" he demanded.

I stammered, "I . . . er . . . you see . . . ah . . ."

Mr. Rogers crossed his arms and stared down at me. "I'm waiting, Theodore."

Mila spoke up. "Great job, Mr. Rogers. You found Jigsaw's worms."

Mr. Rogers grimaced. "Apparently so."

"It's my mistake," Bigs piped up. He handed Mr. Rogers the bag with Ms. Gleason's pumpkin pie. "I brought the wrong bag."

"And these worms?" Mr. Rogers asked.

How could I ever explain it, I wondered.

Mila thought quick. "They're for Jigsaw's costume!" Mila reached into the box and

pulled out a worm. She placed it on my head.

Then Bigs grabbed a few and laid them on my shoulders.

"It adds to the overall creepiness," Mila explained.

Now it was Mr. Rogers's turn to stand in silence.

"Like in the poem," Mila said.

"Poem?"

"Yes, you know:

'The worms go in, the worms go out.
They crawl in your stomach
And out through your mouth.'"

Mr. Rogers rubbed his eyes and groaned.

"I'll get the aspirin," Mrs. Garcia offered.

"Yes, thank you, that would be nice," Mr. Rogers said to her. He turned back to us. "As for you three. Please get back to your classroom, it's nearly time for the parade. And I've got one more pie to taste."

We started to leave.

"Wait!" Mr. Rogers called out. "Please take the worms. Unless they are students here, they don't belong in school."

Chapter Twelve

Joey's Big Moment

The Halloween parade was a gigantic success. All the parents cheered and waved. Cameras flashed. Camcorders whirred. Both my parents were there . . . and so was Grams, waving wildly.

When we got back to room 201 after our march around the school, it was time for the class party. We ate spider cupcakes, opened treat bags, played games, and listened to music.

Everyone turned to look when Mr. Rogers burst through the door. Smiling happily, he handed Ms. Gleason a blue ribbon. She won first prize in the contest! We all clapped and cheered.

At long last, Ms. Gleason let us go outside for afternoon recess. Here was the moment we'd been waiting for.

Eddie Becker clapped Joey on the back. "Nearly everybody bought a ticket," he said. "We're going to be rich!"

We crowded into a tight circle. Joey selected a worm from the box. It was short but thick.

Joey looked at Bobby. "Show me the money," he said.

Mila made a face. "You couldn't pay me a million dollars to eat one of those things."

Ralphie Jordan volunteered. "For a million dollars," he said, "I'd eat a hundred of those suckers."

Bobby held out a portrait of George Washington. Joey reached for the money.

Bobby caught him by the wrist. "No swallowing it whole," he said. "I want to see you chew."

Lucy Hiller turned green.

Nicole Rodriguez turned away.

"Do it, Joey!" Mike Radcliffe urged.

"I need something to wash it down with," Joey Pignattano said. I was prepared for that. I handed Joey a juice box.

"Joey, don't!" Danika said. "That's a living creature."

Joey scratched his head. "It's just a worm," he replied.

"So," Danika said. "Worms are people, too. That little guy has a mom and dad just like you. How do you think they'll feel when they find out that their son was eaten by a second-grader?"

"Who asked you, Danika?" Bobby shot back. "This is between Joey and me."

Danika shook her head sadly. "That little fella's probably got a name. Like Slimy or Slippy or something."

Joey poked at the worm with his finger. "Hi, Slippy," he said. "Are you ticklish?"

"Enough!" Bobby demanded. "Eat it or give my money back."

Joey looked at Danika. "Sorry," he said. "But this is business."

Joey opened his mouth. The worm dangled above his tongue.

And he ate it.

Three chews and a swallow.

He actually ate it.

I was right. It wasn't something you see every day. And that's probably a good thing.

Yuck!

After school, I split the dollar with Mila, fifty-fifty, and we went trick-or-treating around the neighborhood. We saw witches and ghosts, hoboes and tramps. But we didn't see any more mummies.

That was fine with me. I'd already seen enough for one day.

And as they say in the detective business . . . that *wraps* up another case for Jigsaw Jones!